The G[...]
Ghost Guide

By Jenny Alexander

CHAPTER ONE
THE SECRET DOOR

James got out of the car and took a deep breath.
He couldn't see the sea, but he could smell it, and
he could hear the waves breaking on the beach.
The holiday cottage was in a steep lane. He
watched as the lights went on in the windows,
one by one.

Dad was getting the bags out of the boot and taking them into the house. He had to stoop to get through the low front door. Suddenly, a window flew open, and Alice stuck her head out.

"I'm having this room!" she yelled down at James.

The room Alice wanted had pink wallpaper and a flowery bedspread. James preferred the smaller room she had left for him. It had white walls and a sloping ceiling.

Alice came bounding in. "I'm glad you like this room," she said. "I thought you would. After all, it is the one with the secret door!"

She pointed to a low, white-painted door, partly hidden behind a chest of drawers.

"Secret door!" scoffed James. "What is it? An empty cupboard?"

He lifted the latch and peered in. It was pitch dark. There was a torch hanging on a hook behind the door. He looked at Alice.

"Go on!" she said.

He switched on the torch. Now they could see some stairs going steeply up inside the wall.

"What's up there?" James asked.

"How would I know?" said Alice. "You don't think I'd have gone up on my own, do you?"

James went up the stairs, lighting the way with the torch. Alice was right behind him. They found themselves in an attic room. He shone the torch around, and the beam of light came to rest on the only piece of furniture – a cupboard.

"It's like the dark, dark room in the story," Alice whispered. "With the dark, dark cupboard. Do you think there's anything inside it?"

"There's only one way to see," said James. He opened the door.

The cupboard was empty except for a big, old book. It was black, with gold lettering on the front that glimmered in the torchlight. James handed the torch to Alice and took the book out. It was sticky with cobwebs, and he dropped it in disgust. It hit the bare floorboards with a loud BANG!

Alice shot back down the stairs in a flash, with
James hard at her heels. They burst into the
bedroom and slammed the door behind them.
Then they looked at each other and laughed.
Fancy being spooked by an old book in a dusty attic!

But when Alice had gone, James pushed the chest of drawers right up against the secret door. And when he was lying in bed, trying to get to sleep, he thought he might have preferred the room with the pink wallpaper and the flowery bedspread after all.

CHAPTER TWO
FISHING FOR GHOSTS

The attic was a lot less spooky in the daytime. The
sunlight streamed up the stairs from the room
below. The book was lying on the floor in front of
the open cupboard. James knelt down and brushed
the cobwebs off the cover. Now he could read the
gold lettering on the front. It said, "The Good Ghost
Guide".

He was just about to open it when he heard his mum calling him.

"James! Aren't you ready yet? We're all waiting!"

He remembered he was supposed to be getting ready to go to the beach. He went back down to his bedroom and threw his swimming things into a bag. He put "The Good Ghost Guide" in on top of them.

When they got to the beach, the first thing they did was go for a swim. Then they went to get some freshly-baked doughnuts from the beach shop. By that time, their mum had got stuck into her murder mystery and their dad was snoring in the sunshine.

James opened the book. The pages were thick and crisp. It was a list of places around Port Perrigan where you could go and look for ghosts. James found a page called "Port Perrigan Bay".

"That's where we are," Alice said, sprinkling his shoulder with sugar.

They read it together.

Port Perrigan Bay

The ghost of Mad Jack

Mad Jack was a giant of a man, over seven feet tall, with orange hair as thick as a lion's mane. He turned up in Port Perrigan in the summer of 1879, and stayed for eleven years. No one ever found out where he came from or what his real name was because he never spoke.

One day, he went into the cave at the end of Port Perrigan Bay and just sat there, waiting for the tide to come in.

Mad Jack was never seen again, but lots of people claim to have seen his ghost, still sitting there in the back of the cave, waiting for the tide ...

The cave is known as Mad Jack's cavern to this day.

James shut the book. He said to Alice, "Fancy a bit of fishing?"

She screwed up her nose. "No way!" she said. "Fishing's boring."

"Not the kind of fishing I've got in mind," said James. "I'm thinking of fishing for ghosts!"

Chapter Three
Mad Jack's Cavern

The mouth of the cave was low and narrow, and they had to bend down to go inside. Then it opened up like a tunnel. The sandy floor was damp and cold, after the warmth of the beach. They came to a wide, shallow pool and began to paddle through it.

It was quite dark up ahead. The surface of the
water looked like grey silk in the gloom, and big
drops splashed into the pool from the roof of
the cave.

At the far side, they stopped. Looking back, they
could see the sunlight coming in through the mouth
of the cave, dancing on the water. Looking ahead,
there was nothing but darkness.

"I don't like this," said Alice. Her voice
came echoing back.

There was a strange, sucking noise behind them, like water running down a plughole. They spun round. The pool was turning, like a whirlpool. The air was suddenly sucked down into it with a great whooshing noise. Alice grabbed James's arm.

But as suddenly as it had started, it stopped. The water became calm again, and the only sound was the plop-plop of drips falling into it from the roof above.

James and Alice splashed back through the pool and ran down the long tunnel. They crawled out onto the beach and threw themselves down on the sand.

"That was horrible!" cried Alice. "I was really scared."

James frowned. "We mustn't let our imaginations run away with us," he said. "I mean, we didn't see a ghost, did we? There's probably a simple explanation for what we saw."

They started walking back along the beach.

"I think we should look in the book and try another one," said James.

Alice didn't agree. "I say we put the book back and forget about it," she said.

When they got back to the blanket, Alice picked up her spade and went to join some other girls who were making dams by the water's edge. James opened "The Good Ghost Guide".

Port Perrigan

The Old Manor Inn

Years ago, the Old Manor was the home of Sir Barnaby Bracewell and his wife, Lady Grace. They had five beautiful daughters.

One day, Sir Barnaby was riding home from hunting when the housekeeper's cat ran under his horse's hooves and was killed.

But what haunts the Old Manor now is not the housekeeper's cat ... It is everyone else. For the housekeeper took revenge on Sir Barnaby by putting poison in his wine, and he shared it with his wife and daughters.

They all died. But they had been so happy together in the Old Manor that they have never left it.

In recent years, the Old Manor has become a pub. Many visitors have called in for a quiet drink, only to hear the ghosts of the Bracewell family pacing up and down in the corridor above.

"Tell you what," said James's dad, waking up.
"Why don't we all pop into a pub for a quiet drink
before supper?"

CHAPTER FOUR
THE GHOST CODE

The Old Manor Inn had a garden overlooking the beach. James and Alice sat down at one of the tables while their mum and dad went inside to buy some drinks. James told Alice about the housekeeper's cat, and the ghosts.

"We could just have a look," he suggested.

"Are you kidding?" she said.

"OK, then. Tell Mum and Dad I've gone to the loo."

He went in the side door and found himself in a hallway. There were some stairs on the left, with a sign saying "Residents Only Beyond This Point". He made sure there was nobody watching, and then ran silently up them.

He found himself in a corridor. The setting sun was streaming in through a tall window at the far end. It filled the corridor with soft, red light. There was no sign of any ghosts.

It started as a breath of cold air, that sprinkled his
skin with goose pimples. Then a rush of wind
swept along the empty corridor. The curtains
billowed and the lightshades swayed. James held
on to the banisters as the wind ripped through his
clothes and pulled at his hair. After a few moments,
it stopped.

Alice didn't ask him if he had seen anything and
he didn't tell her. He wanted to think things
through on his own. Maybe water in caves
sometimes started to spin – he didn't know; he
didn't know much about caves at all. But he knew
howling gales didn't go ripping through corridors
when all the windows and doors were shut.

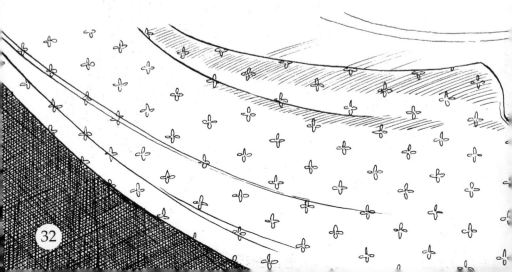

When they got home, he went straight to his room and unpacked his beach bag. He sat with "The Good Ghost Guide" in his hands. He hadn't seen Mad Jack or Sir Barnaby Bracewell, but weird things had certainly happened. A voice behind him said, "It was me."

James turned his head. He saw a smudge of yellow light hovering above the window seat. As he watched, it got clearer like a picture coming into focus. The yellow light was a bead of amber on a black string, and the string was tied round the neck of a pale, pale boy. He had shoulder-length fair hair and he was wearing shorts and sandals, as if he had come straight from the beach.

"H-how did you get in?" James stammered.

The boy threw back his head and laughed. But his laugh sounded faint and far away. His body faded until he was no more than mist around the yellow glow of the amber bead.

"You're a ghost!" whispered James.

The boy reappeared. "That's right," he agreed.

"But you aren't in 'The Good Ghost Guide'."

"You don't understand," said the ghost. "'The Good Ghost Guide' isn't a guide for people to find ghosts. It's a guide for ghosts to find people. We aren't allowed just to appear to someone without so much as a by your leave. It wouldn't be safe. They might drop down dead in fright. We have to make sure we only show ourselves to people who aren't scared. That's the Ghost Code."

"There isn't really a Mad Jack, or a Sir Barnaby Bracewell. It was all a test. Your sister flunked it, but you passed with flying colours. You passed because when I threw in a few cold winds, you still came back for more."

"So you wanted to appear to us," said James. "But why?"

"Because I think you can do something for me," said the ghost.

CHAPTER FIVE
THE MESSAGE

"I've got this friend," said the ghost. "He's called Matt. You'll like him."

James closed his eyes, but when he opened them again, the ghost was still there. How was it possible, if ghosts were only allowed to appear to people who weren't scared?

"I don't think I want to meet any more ghosts," he said.

"Matt isn't a ghost. He's alive and kicking. Well, alive and fishing right now, I should think. I want you to give him a message.

"Matt was with me on the day I ... the day it happened. We were playing chicken on the rocks under the cliff. We saw this enormous wave coming, and Matt legged it. But I hung on.

"The wave knocked me off my feet and swept me into the water. Matt ran to get the lifebelt from the lookout hut. But by the time he got back, it was too late. He just stood there, hugging the lifebelt to his chest, with tears streaming down his face.

"The problem is, he blames himself for what happened. He thinks he should have jumped in after me. But then he'd just have drowned as well.

"I want you to tell him you've seen me. Tell him it wasn't his fault. It was just me being stupid. Tell him to stop being so hard on himself, and start being happy again."

James went down to the beach. The sky was dark, and there was a thin mist rolling in from the sea. The edge of the water was a thin white line, with fishermen dotted along it.

He didn't know what Matt looked like, but he couldn't ask because the ghost had gone. Then he saw him. A boy about the same age as himself, with dark curly hair, bending over to bait his line.

"Are you Matt?" said James.

The boy looked round. He didn't look very friendly.

"Who's asking?"

James took a deep breath. "I've got a message for you from your friend," he said. "The one who drowned."

He blurted out the whole story – about "The Good Ghost Guide", and the amber bead, and the message he had to bring. When he had finished, Matt just sat there, staring at him. Then he said, "I didn't jump in because I was scared."

"But you did the right thing," said James. "You did the sensible thing. Now there's something that I've got to do."

He walked away across the sand. He was going to get "The Good Ghost Guide" and put it back where it came from.

But when he got to his bedroom, "The Good Ghost Guide" had gone.